D0586837

This book belongs to

Sugarplum
Mines

The
Lak

Zuckerbrote
Peak

Donkey's Causeway

Drosselmeyer P

The
Rocks

The Western Frostings

Dros

The

Rocky
Falls

King Caspar's Mines

Rushing River

Leopard's Paradise

ns

The City The Forest

neyer Plains

Valley

R. Verbena

Toffee-Apple Orchards

The Eastern Frosting

*Look out for all the Kingdom
of the Frosty Mountains books!*

KINGDOM OF THE
FROSTY MOUNTAINS

Jessica Juniper

Emerald Everhart

Illustrated by
Patricia Ann Lewis-MacDougall

EGMONT

EGMONT

We bring stories to life

Jessica Juniper first published in 2008
by Egmont UK Limited
239 Kensington High Street
London W8 6SA

Text copyright © 2008 Angela Woolfe
Illustrations copyright © 2008 Patricia Ann Lewis-MacDougall

The moral rights of the author and illustrator have been asserted

ISBN 978 1 4052 3326 2

1 3 5 7 9 10 8 6 4 2

A CIP catalogue record for this title is available from the British Library

Printed and bound in Italy by L.E.G.O. S.P.A

Contents

Prologue

When I was a young Ballerina, an admirer gave me a gift.

It was only a frosted-glass perfume bottle, filled with a sweet scent of lemon and orange. But my admirer told me that

the bottle was the most precious thing he could give, because there was a magical Kingdom inside.

I didn't believe him at first.

But that night, I had a very special dream. I dreamed of a magical Kingdom, the most beautiful land I'd ever seen, filled with delightful people and their very special animals. And the next time I danced, I thought of the Kingdom, and suddenly I danced as I had never danced before. Every night that I wore the perfume, I danced better than ever, until I was the most famous ballerina in the world.

But one day, the old frosted-glass bottle was accidentally thrown away.

And from that day onwards, I never danced so beautifully again.

I searched for the bottle high and low, but I never found it. I have since had many years to write down what I learned about the Kingdom inside . . .

Inside the bottle, behind snow-capped Frosty Mountains, the Kingdom is divided

into five parts. There are frozen Lakes in the north, warmer meadows in the southern Valley, stark grey Rocks in the west, and to the east, a deep, dark Forest.

And the City. How could I forget the City? Silverberg, the capital, rising from the

Drosselmeyer Plains like a beautiful new jewel on an old ring.

From a distance, the houses seem to be piled on top of each other. Their brightly painted wooden roofs look as if they hold up the floors of the dwellings above as they wind around and around ever-more-narrow streets. And at the very top of the teetering pile is the biggest building of all: the Royal Palace. It is made from snow-white marble taken from the Frosty Mountains themselves, which glows in

the early morning sun and sparkles in the
cold night.

    The Royal Palace is the home of the
King and Queen. But it is here too, within

the marble walls of the Palace, that you can find the Kingdom's famous Royal Ballet School. This is where the most talented young Ballerinas in the land become proper Ballerinas-in-Training, and really learn to dance. They travel from far and wide. Pale blonde Lake girls journey from the north, dark-haired Valley Dwellers come from the south. Grey-eyed Ballerinas travel from the western Rocks, and green-eyed Forest girls make their way from the east. The City girls have no need to come quite so far.

Of course, they all bring their pets. Each Kingdom Dweller has their own animal companion. And these animals can talk — talk just like you and me. Lake Dwellers keep Arctic foxes or snow leopards, while Valley Dwellers keep small tigers, monkeys or exotic birds. Strong, sturdy Rock Dwellers enjoy the company of sheep, goats and donkeys, while Forest Dwellers keep black bears and leopards. Every City Dweller keeps an eagle.

Out there, somewhere, is my old

frosted-glass perfume bottle.

Out there, somewhere, are the Ballerinas-in-Training who inspired me — Jessica Juniper, Crystal Coldwater, Laura-Bella Bergamotta, Valentina de la Frou and Ursula of the Boughs.

And they will wait for you, until the day that you find them.

Emerald Everhart

CHAPTER ONE
A New Start

It isn't easy to leave your home. It isn't easy to leave your mother and father and your eight brothers and sisters to go to boarding school in a faraway city.

But just after sunrise on a chilly

autumn morning, somewhere in the west of the Kingdom of the Frosty Mountains, Jessica Juniper was about to do just that.

And she was very, very excited.

She did not know how she'd feel if she were setting off all by herself to an ordinary school, to learn maths and reading and geography. But Jessica Juniper had won a place at the famous Royal Ballet School, where she would become a Ballerina-in-Training.

Besides, she was not all alone. Sinbad,

her pet donkey, was going with her.

'Goodbye, Mother Juniper! Goodbye, Father Juniper! Goodbye, Jemima, Jennifer, Jeremiah, Joseph, Jezebel, Janice, Josiah and Jimmy!' Sinbad waved his long brown ears that stuck out from holes in his woolly hat, and bellowed so loudly at the enormous Juniper family gathered beside their tiny house that Jessica completely forgot about the lump in her throat.

'Ssshh, Sinbad, you'll wake the neighbours!' Jessica loved her donkey, but

she did sometimes wish he didn't make so much noise. 'Bye, House!' she called more quietly. 'Bye, everyone! We'll see you soon.' She brushed a tear from her eyes and set off down the garden path.

'Goodbye, Sally Sheep!' Sinbad hollered at the other family pets. 'Goodbye, Billy Goat!'

'Goodbye, Jessica! Goodbye, Sinbad! We'll miss you.' Jessica's enormous family all waved, jumping up and down to see over each other's heads.

'They'll miss me!' Sinbad wailed, hurrying after Jessica. He wobbled as he trotted along, because of the battered suitcase that was strapped around his

large middle. It was filled with a few of Jessica's clothes, and *all* of Sinbad's hats.

'Isn't this amazing, Sinbad?' Jessica gave a little pirouette, liking the way her pink uniform floated as she moved. It was nearly new, bought from an older girl in the village, and it was the most beautiful dress Jessica had ever owned. Her soft grey Rock-Dweller's cloak was nearly new too, with her name embroidered on the edge. 'We're off on an adventure!'

Sinbad frowned. 'Are you *sure* we're doing the right thing, Jess?'

'Of course!' Jessica had held this conversation many times since winning her place, both with Sinbad and in her own head. 'I've always dreamed of this,

Sinbad. If I work very hard, maybe one day I'll be a famous dancer, like Aurora Rosmarino, or even Eva Snowdrop!'

'And then you'll forget all about me!' Sinbad stopped. 'I can't let that happen. Let's stay here in the Rocks, where it's safe, and where I'll always be your best friend!'

'Sinbad, you'll always be my best friend wherever we are,' said Jessica.

'But it's an awfully long journey to Silverberg.' Sinbad stared out at the stony path. 'There might be bandits . . .' – his eyes widened – '. . . giants . . .' – his eyes widened even further – '*dragons*!'

Jessica sighed. 'There's no such thing as giants, or dragons, Sinbad.'

'But I've heard stories all about them!'

'Sinbad, you've *told* stories all about them.' Jessica knew how the donkey loved to gather the other pets around the fire and tell fairy tales.

'*And* the city is full of thieves . . . *and*

you get executed for doing the slightest thing wrong!'

Jessica had never been to Silverberg, but she knew that Sinbad was making this up. 'It's going to be wonderful,' she said. 'Dancing every day, and making new friends, and midnight feasts . . .'

'Midnight feasts?' gasped Sinbad, setting off again as fast as he could. 'Well, why didn't you say so?'

Jessica and Sinbad scampered down the sharp grey Rocks like only Rock

Dwellers can, and then began the trek across the wind swept Drosselmeyer Plains. The light began to brighten the view to the east, and soon Silverberg itself was visible in the distance. The shimmering marble Palace glowed white in the morning sun.

'What do you think of our adventure now, Sinbad?'

Sinbad could not speak for once. And he remained silent until they reached Silverberg's West Gate. High above them, the Palace bells were chiming eight o'clock.

'Here we are,' said Jessica.

'Help me put my new hat on!' Sinbad shook off his woolly hat. 'I can't arrive without my smart City hat, Jessica!'

Jessica opened the suitcase and pulled out a black bowler with a fresh flower in the brim. Then, putting it on Sinbad's head, she led him through the West Gate.

CHAPTER TWO
The Golden Carriage

The narrow street ahead was filled with shouts and clattering, as the strangest people Jessica had ever seen went about their business.

The City Dwellers wore vivid red

velvet cloaks, mustard-yellow stockings and shiny purple buckled shoes. They all wore very elaborate hats that made Sinbad's precious new bowler look shabby and old-fashioned, and each person carried an eagle on their shoulder. The City Dwellers' skin was softer than the country people Jessica knew, their hair more carefully styled and the air around them more perfumed.

They were all busy shopping. They paused at the street stalls selling sticky fruits. They lingered at stalls of fresh-baked bread and cakes. And they held their noses as they hurried past a stall that advertised 'MOULDY AND ROTTEN VEG FOR YOUR COMPOST HEAP!!'

'*Wow!*' said Sinbad. 'Wow, wow and *triple* wow!' Then he noticed a delicious scent. 'Jessica! Cinnamon Twists! Where's that lovely smell coming from . . . ?'

Suddenly, Jessica felt a shove to her back. 'Move, country bumpkins!' a voice snapped.

She turned to see a thin man in a black hat scowling down at her from an enormous height. For a moment she thought Sinbad had been right about the giants after all. Then she realised that the man was sitting on the front of a gleaming golden carriage. In the City fashion, the carriage had no wheels, but was held up at each end by two burly carriage-bearers.

'I said, move!' the man repeated, kicking a mustard-yellow-stockinged leg at Jessica. His eagle glared. 'Don't you know who this carriage belongs to?'

'We're new in town,' Jessica began.

'Well, it belongs to Chancellor Goodfellow, the most important man in the land. His daughter is travelling inside. All hail the precious Miss Rubellina!'

'*Wow!*' said Sinbad. 'Can I get an autograph?'

Mustard Stockings ignored him. 'And *I* am the Chancellor's nephew. Move from our path, Commoners. We're in a hurry to get to the Royal Ballet School.'

'That's where we're going!' said Jessica. 'Can I say hello to Rubellina?'

'Not unless you want me to pinch you,' snapped Mustard Stockings.

'Move!' came a voice from the carriage. It was Rubellina herself. The eagle

on her shoulder scowled at Jessica, and squawked noisily.

Jessica recognised her long, curly hair and sharp eyes from the gossip magazines her sisters loved.

'And move that stinky old donkey,' Rubellina added.

'Hey!' Sinbad protested. 'I'm not stinky!'

'Well, you're not *old*,' mumbled Jessica, moving Sinbad. If the other Ballerinas were like Rubellina, she was not at all sure that she and Sinbad were going to fit in.

Suddenly they heard a call from a plump woman carrying a steaming tray. 'Hot Cinnamon Twists, freshest in Silverberg!'

'Cinnamon Twists!' Sinbad started running towards the woman. Then he heard another shout from another tradesman, further up the street.

'Hot Cinnamon Twists, finest in Silverberg!'

'*Finest* Cinnamon Twists!' Sinbad skidded to a stop, unsure which stall to choose.

'Hot Cinnamon Twists,' shouted a third trader from his stall opposite, '*biggest* in Silverberg!'

This was the magic word.

Sinbad ran towards the third stall. His hind legs accidentally kicked Rubellina's golden carriage, which began

to tip slowly sideways.

Rubellina and Mustard Stockings shrieked, their eagles squawked, and the carriage crashed to the cobbles, spilling them all into a nearby stall.

A very particular stall.

The MOULDY AND ROTTEN VEG FOR YOUR COMPOST HEAP stall.

All the market-traders came running over.

'Arrest that girl! Arrest that donkey!' screamed Mustard Stockings.

'I *told* you we'd be executed, Jessica!' gasped Sinbad. 'Run!'

But Jessica was trying to help Rubellina get up. 'I'm sorry, Rubellina!' she began. 'It was an accident –'

'An *accident?*' Rubellina's red cloak had fallen into a heap of stinking cabbages, her stockings were stained with cauliflower slime, and her hat was torn. 'I'll make sure you're thrown out of Ballet School!'

Her eagle let out a furious squawk of agreement. 'You'll be *expelled* before you've even started!' he hissed.

'There's no need to be mean,' said a tall girl on the edges of the crowd. She had the ice-blue eyes and light hair of a Lake Dweller, and a small Arctic fox peered out from her cloak. 'It *was* an accident, Rubellina. Besides, nothing's broken.'

'Not *broken*?' Rubellina brandished her ruined hat.

'No bones are broken,' said another

girl in the crowd, who was stroking Sinbad's shaking ears. She was a tiny, dark-haired Valley Dweller, wearing an odd mixture of pink Ballet School uniform and thick yellow sweaters.

One of the market traders dared to join in, despite the presence of the Chancellor's daughter. 'Well, yes, I agree,' he said, bravely. 'There's no call to threaten the girl, *or* her poor smelly donkey.'

Sinbad stopped shaking, and glared.

'She's far from home, poor thing . . . alone in the big city . . .' Everyone was now on Jessica's side.

Mustard Stockings and Rubellina had heard quite enough. As haughtily as they knew how, they clambered back into the carriage. Mustard-Stockings kicked the carriage-bearers, who started off towards the Palace.

'Hey! You've left your cloak . . .' Jessica pulled Rubellina's cloak from the cabbages, but by the time she turned round, the carriage was gone. Jessica turned to the two girls. 'Thank you. You really stood up for me.'

'Well, Ballerinas have to stick together! I'm a Beginner at the School, too,' said the Valley Dweller. She was so tiny that she had to look up at them both. 'My name's Laura-Bella Bergamotta.'

'I'm Jessica Juniper!' Jessica was feeling better.

'Call me Crys,' joined in the tall Lake Dweller. She pointed at the name

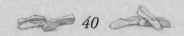

Crystal Coldwater embroidered on her cloak. 'Nobody *ever* calls me Crystal. And this is my fox, Pollux. He doesn't say much, but he's terribly clever.'

The little white fox nodded at them all, and twitched his whiskers in greeting.

'My donkey's called Sinbad.' Jessica pointed to Sinbad, who was helping himself to mouthfuls of spilled Cinnamon Twists. 'He says a *lot*. Where's your pet, Laura-Bella?'

'Over there, about to scold your

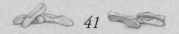

donkey for raiding the stalls. His name's Mr Melchior.'

Jessica saw a small tiger stalk up to Sinbad and tap him on the hindquarters with a stern paw. The donkey turned

around, glimpsed the tiger's teeth, and dropped every one of the twelve Cinnamon Twists stuffed in his mouth.

'Mr Melchior is so *proper*,' laughed Laura-Bella. 'He wants me to smarten my uniform, but it's so cold here compared to back home, I need my sweaters. You'd better watch out, or he'll boss you about, too!'

Jessica liked the sound of this. It sounded as though Laura-Bella wanted to stay friends. She stuffed Rubellina's cloak into her satchel, to return later. 'We'd better hurry. The Welcoming Ceremony starts at nine o'clock!'

CHAPTER THREE
The Welcoming Ceremony

The Great Hall, inside the Royal Palace, was the biggest room Jessica had ever seen, and quite the most magnificent. Every surface was Frostings marble, inlaid with gold. The ceiling was so high that she had to crane her neck to see it properly. All around, the older girls chatted together, pleased to see their friends after the holidays, but the twenty-one new Beginners were less relaxed.

Jessica saw Rubellina talking to two other Beginners, and went over.

'I've brought your cloak, Rubellina,' she smiled. 'I'm sorry about the accident. Can we be friends?'

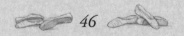 *46*

Rubellina tossed her head, and her eagle copied the gesture. 'Not likely,' she said. 'You have to be *very* special to be my friend.'

'But Jessica *is* very special,' Sinbad said. 'She's kind, and funny, and great at telling bedtime stories – not *quite* as good as me, but I'm the best ever. Ooooh, maybe I could be your friend

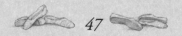 *47*

too, and tell you stories, and have midnight feasts, and . . .'

'Does your donkey ever stop talking?' Rubellina interrupted, nudging the girls beside her. The one on her left, a City Dweller, stared at Jessica and Sinbad as though she would like to scrape them off her shoe. The name *Jo-Jo Marshall* was embroidered on her red cloak. The dark-haired girl on Rubellina's right stared shyly downwards, clinging to her small black bear. The wonky letters on her

green cloak read *Ursula of the Boughs.*

Rubellina snatched her cloak back and put it on. 'I'm not even sure Rock Dwellers are good enough to be at the

Ballet School, but I'll let you know if I decide to like you or not.'

'Surely *we* ought to decide whether we like *her* or not,' Sinbad hissed, as Jessica pulled him back to their row. 'She insulted Rock Dwellers! How can you hold your tongue?'

'I don't want to make enemies,' said Jessica, as she slipped into line between Crys and Laura-Bella. Then she spotted the teachers, all seated up on a platform. Jessica recognised the two who had come to the Rocks to audition her: Mistress Hawthorne, the jolly gym mistress, and the stern Head, Mistress Odette, who taught ballet.

'I hope Mistress Odette isn't teaching *us*,' she whispered to Crys and Laura-Bella.

'She only teaches the older girls,' said a voice.

Jessica turned round to look at the City Dweller who had just spoken behind her. *Valentina de la Frou* was

embroidered on her red cloak. Although she was just as stylish as Rubellina, with waist-length fair hair tied in shiny red ribbons, her face was very friendly, and her eagle looked nice.

'Hi,' said the eagle. 'I'm Olympia,

and this is Valentina!'

'I'm Jessica, and this is my donkey Sinbad. Are you Second Years?'

'No, Beginners too,' said Valentina. 'But my dad works here at the Palace, so he tells me about all the teachers. I don't know *that* one, though.'

She pointed at the platform. In the back row, his large black hat mostly hiding his face, sat Mustard Stockings.

'He's a *teacher*?' Jessica groaned.

Suddenly, they all heard a loud noise.

'It's the Seventeen Royal Flugelhorns!' said Valentina.

Seventeen musicians now entered the Hall, all dressed in white velvet. On their shoulders sat their special musical eagles, quietly cawing to prepare their voices for song.

'This means the King and Queen will be here any minute,' hissed Valentina.

As she spoke, the Flugelhorns began a glorious fanfare.

'Wow!' Sinbad breathed. 'I have *got*

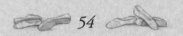 54

to get one of those flugelhorns.'

Jessica did not tell Sinbad that he made quite enough noise already.

Then the musical eagles began to sing, their voices soaring.

'*Wow!*' said Sinbad. 'I have *got* to get one of those eagles.'

King Caspar led the Royal Procession. His golden cloak was so spectacular that you hardly noticed that the King himself looked like a very dozy dormouse. His eagle was fast asleep.

Queen Mab, on the other hand, looked rather fierce. Her hair was piled so high that it made her almost twice as tall as the King, and her crown dripped with glittering Frosting-Crystals. Her eagle was the plumpest bird Jessica had ever seen.

Finally came Rubellina's father, Chancellor Goodfellow. He walked tall in his robes of black and gold, his thin lips forming a chilly smile. On his shoulder was a tiny eagle with sharp talons.

The fanfare ended, and everyone

sat down.

'Well, well, well,' said the King, patting his robe for his spectacles. 'How . . . er . . . nice to see you back for another . . . er . . . term. Now, I must give a . . . er . . . special welcome to . . . ' The King stopped. 'D'you know, I've completely forgotten what I was supposed to say.'

'Twerp!' snapped Queen Mab.

'Maybe my . . . er . . . Keeper of the Lists will know. De la Frou!' called the King.

A man hurried in, covered in ink and wrestling a bundle of huge paper scrolls.

Behind Jessica, Valentina de la Frou groaned. 'That's my dad. *How* embarrassing.'

'What is on today's List?' asked the King.

Mr de la Frou unrolled a scroll. 'Item one, Wake Up,' he said.

'Well, I'm *certain* I did that.' The King looked pleased.

'Item two, Eat Breakfast.'

'Did *that* too! A very tasty Raspberry Flancake, to be . . . er . . . precise. Or was that . . . er . . . yesterday . . . ?'

The King fell silent, trying to remember. His eagle began to snore.

'Oh, dear, dear. It's just the same as last year.' The Head, Mistress Odette, patted the King's arm, and stepped forward. 'Welcome, everyone,' she said, 'especially the Beginners. I know you'll be very happy here. Now, I have one or two announcements. A new teacher is joining Mistress Camomile in the Ballet department – Master Lysander.'

Mustard Stockings stood and bowed.

Jessica met her new friends' eyes and saw that they were thinking the same thing – *Please don't let him be our teacher.*

'. . . no running in the corridors, *no*

feeding the musical eagles . . .' Mistress Odette was looking more stern than ever. 'Remember also, girls, that last term we were bothered by some tiresome practical jokes – Third Years, you know who I mean!'

Several of the Third Years stared at their feet.

'It is *not* funny to dip hair ribbons in itching powder. It is *not* funny to fill your friends' ballet shoes with cranberry custard.'

'Actually, I think that *is* quite funny,' Sinbad whispered.

'This term, a Black Mark will be given to anyone who plays a practical joke,' Mistress Odette said. 'And you all know how serious a Black Mark is.'

'Three of them in one term and you get expelled,' whispered Valentina.

'Finally, Beginners, auditions for your End-of-term Ballet take place next week. The ballet will be *Cinderella*.'

Cinderella! Jessica wondered if she

had any chance of a good part.

'Mistress Odette, could I add something?' Smooth as silk, Chancellor Goodfellow turned to the King and Queen. 'It is not just my nephew, Master Lysander, who is joining the School. Most High Majesties, may I present my beloved daughter?'

Rubellina flounced towards the platform.

'Oh, no!' Jessica froze.

A scrap of paper was stuck to

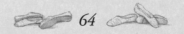

Rubellina's cloak.

It was part of the sign from the vegetable stall.

'MOULDY AND ROTTEN,' said the words on Rubellina's back.

CHAPTER FOUR
Black Mark

Everyone in the Hall had seen the sign. People began to giggle as Rubellina swept into a curtsey.

'Charming, charming,' said the Queen. 'Show the High Majesties your

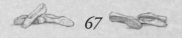

pirouette, Rubellina,' said the Chancellor.

Rubellina performed a pirouette that would have been perfect if not for the words MOULDY AND ROTTEN on her back.

'What a very . . . er . . . unusual name,' said the King. 'Do you shorten it to Mouldy, my dear?'

Mistress Odette removed the sign from Rubellina's back. 'What is this, Rubellina?'

Rubellina saw the words, and screamed.

'*Outrage!*' Chancellor Goodfellow's face was purple. 'Who is responsible?'

'Don't say anything, Jess!' hissed Sinbad. 'We'll be executed now, I just know it!'

But Jessica stood, legs shaking. 'It wasn't meant to happen . . . in the accident . . .'

'*Rock Dweller!*' bellowed the Chancellor. 'Rubellina told me about you . . .'

'Quiet, Godwin!' Mistress Odette's

voice was not loud, but the Chancellor stopped speaking immediately. 'Jessica, I'm rather disappointed. You seemed such a sensible girl. This is unfortunate, but rules are rules. A practical joke means a Black Mark.'

Jessica felt her eyes sting, but she would not cry in front of the whole school. Sinbad had no such determination, however, and began to wail softly.

'The right decision, Head Mistress,' purred Chancellor Goodfellow.

Mistress Odette shot him an irritable glance. 'Well, girls, on a jollier note, there is a Welcome Feast in the Banquet Hall. White Chocolate Meringues *and* Cook's famous Cinnamon Twists!'

The entire school stampeded for the Banquet Hall.

'They'll be expelled – the stinky donkey *and* the Rock girl.' Rubellina swept past, talking loudly to Jo-Jo and Ursula. 'Wait and see.'

'Ignore her, Jessica,' Valentina said.

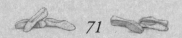

'You need to get *three* Black Marks in one term to be expelled, and even the *worst* pupil has never got more than one.'

'Then I'll have to be so good that I don't get any more!' said Jessica, forcing herself to smile. 'Let's go and cheer ourselves up with Cinnamon Twists!'

It was not the start to Ballet School that Jessica had wanted, but she really hoped that Valentina was right.

CHAPTER FIVE
Life at the Palace

Jessica's first week passed in a blur.

Every day began and ended with Ballet class. Luckily this was not taught by Mustard Stockings, but by kind Mistress Camomile. Jessica was relieved to find that she was just as good as the others, apart from Crys, who was by far the best.

Laura-Bella's best subject was Mime. Pretty blonde Valentina was good at Costume, Hair and Make-up. Crys, though wonderful at Ballet, liked

Gym class best. Her long arms and legs were built for running and jumping.

Pets did not usually attend classes, and Mr Melchior the tiger, Pollux the fox and Olympia the eagle were happy to play together while the girls studied. But Sinbad would not be kept away from the classroom. He adored Gym, even the stretching exercises that wrapped him up in a knot like a pretzel. He loved to clump about at the back in Ballet, and to partner Jessica in

Costume, Hair and Make-up.

'More spray!' he would yell, as Jessica arranged his ears into a fancy style. 'Fluffier! And where's my Easter Bonnet? That's *just* the hat for this ear-do.'

Jessica's favourite class was History of Ballet, taught by Master Silas, the strictest teacher in the school. There were rumours that he had once been a dancer himself, and although he had a terrible limp, his steps were light and graceful. Certainly he could tell wonderful stories about famous Ballerinas that kept even Sinbad quiet.

But Jessica's favourite thing about Ballet School was her three new friends. Every evening they huddled under their pink-and-gold quilts in the cosy dormitory, listening to Sinbad's stories after lights-out, while Mr Melchior tried to get them all to go to sleep. Jessica, Crys, Laura-Bella and Valentina had luckily got beds together, and even more luckily they were far away from Rubellina.

Rubellina had not forgotten or forgiven the MOULDY AND ROTTEN affair. While the other Beginners spent the first week settling in, and making friends, Rubellina spent most of her time giggling nastily about Jessica with Jo-Jo and Ursula. Jo-Jo usually had a spiteful word to add, but Ursula always hid behind her dark fringe. In fact, Jessica couldn't help noticing how frightened Ursula was of Rubellina. Ursula waited hand and foot

on the Chancellor's spoiled daughter at mealtimes, and made her bed for her every morning. She even missed the special Beginners' Welcome Party In the first weekend of term because she was busy doing Rubellina's History homework for her. And neither Ursula nor her bear would accept the slices of Munchmallow Cake that Jessica brought from the party to offer them. It seemed like they were too afraid of Rubellina even to look Jessica in the eye.

It was as if hardly a minute had passed, but as Jessica lay in bed one night during her second week at school, she realised that the auditions for *Cinderella* were tomorrow She knew she'd never get the part of Cinderella herself, but after her Black Mark, it would be wonderful to write home to her family to say that she had a solo part.

Jessica tossed and turned in her bed that night. She had to try her hardest tomorrow, and prove that she was a good pupil after all . . .

CHAPTER SIX
The Auditions

Over breakfast the next morning, Jessica and her friends could hardly touch their Snowberry Muffins. Jessica had even more reason to be nervous, as she had just learned that she was to be the first to audition for *Cinderella*.

'It's all dreadfully nerve-racking,' declared Sinbad, looking not in the least nervous as he polished off his eleventh muffin. 'D'you think I've got any chance of playing the Fairy God-Donkey?'

'Sinbad, it's the Fairy God*mother*! And you can't audition!

Pets aren't allowed.'

The donkey stopped sulking in time to help Jessica warm up before the audition.

'Nervous, Jessica?' Rubellina sneered, warming up nearby. 'Everybody knows you'll get a rotten part, just like everybody knows I'm *bound* to be Cinderella.'

'Ugly Sister, more like,' muttered Sinbad, as Jessica went into the Great Hall.

Mistress Odette was at a long table. Jessica had expected to see Mistress

Camomile and Master Jacques, the Mime teacher, beside her. But, although Master Jacques was there, kind Mistress Camomile was not. Another teacher was in her place. Mustard Stockings.

Jessica stopped, and gulped.

'This will be . . . interesting,' sneered Mustard Stockings.

Jessica said nothing. She scrambled on to the platform, took her position, and waited for a moment.

Then, as the piano-player struck up

the beautiful tune, Jessica started to dance.

She concentrated very hard, determined to prove to Mistress Odette that she was a good pupil, and determined to silence Mustard Stockings. Her polka was perfect. Her jetés were light as air. And she managed a pirouette that even Crys would have been proud of.

When the piano stopped, Jessica was amazed to see Mistress Odette smiling.

'Excellent, Jessica,' she said.

Master Jacques said nothing, but

mimed wiping away a tear with a handkerchief.

'Next!' snapped Mustard Stockings.

Once everyone had auditioned, all the Beginners were called back into the

Hall for the announcement.

Tiny Laura-Bella was to play a mouse, along with Rubellina's two friends, Ursula and Jo-Jo, and Valentina had the part of the chief forest sprite. Once the small solo parts had been announced, Mistress Odette's stern face crinkled into a rare smile.

'Prince Charming will be played by Crystal Coldwater.'

Everyone clapped. It was the most difficult role, and they all knew Crys, the best dancer and the tallest in the class, would get it.

'The Fairy Godmother will be played by Rubellina Goodfellow.'

'*What?* screeched Rubellina.

'And the part of Cinderella goes to Jessica Juniper.'

Everyone gasped.

Jessica stared at Mustard Stockings. 'Are . . . are you *sure?*'

'You danced extremely well,' muttered Mustard Stockings, furiously. 'I could not argue with Mistress Odette.'

The entire class applauded. Even Ursula clapped, until Rubellina pinched her.

'Rehearsals begin tomorrow,' said Mistress Odette. 'And as Mistress Camomile is too busy to direct your show, Master Lysander is in charge instead.'

Jessica's delight gave way to dismay.

But Rubellina had cheered up. She seemed to have forgotten that she had lost the part of Cinderella to the girl she hated.

There was a smile on her face. Her eyes gleamed.

Rubellina Goodfellow was planning something. Something very nasty.

CHAPTER SEVEN
Sewing Trouble

Although Jessica had dreaded rehearsals with Mustard Stockings, he was not nearly so horrible as she had feared. He snapped when she made mistakes, and moaned that she must work harder, but this was not so very different from Jessica's ballet teachers back home.

And Rubellina was as nice as Snowberry Pie.

'Hi, Jess! Hi, Crys!' she would sing out as she saw Jessica and Crys coming towards the studio. 'Here we are again, the three solo stars!' And she would compliment Crys on the hair ribbon that brought out the colour of her ice-blue eyes, or admire Jessica's new leotard.

'Rubellina's all right, really,' Jessica

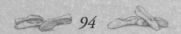

said to Crys one evening.

'Huh!' said Crys, exchanging a glance with Pollux the fox, who said nothing, as usual.

'She's just a bit spoilt because of her dad,' Jessica continued.  'She needs proper friends, who like her for herself.'

Only three days before the show, Jessica was surprised to find Rubellina crying in the changing rooms.

'Rubellina, what's wrong?'

'It's these shoes.' Rubellina pulled out a pair of ballet shoes from her sparkly kitbag, so new that the ribbons had still not been sewn on. 'My old ones hurt, but I can't wear these new ones without ribbons!'

'But sewing's ever so easy,' said Jessica.

'But Nanny always sews on my ribbons at home,' wailed Rubellina. 'And the show's in three days, and I have to sew the ribbons myself, and I don't . . . know . . . how!'

'I'll help you!' said Jessica, smiling.

Rubellina stopped sobbing. 'Really? You'll sew my ribbons on for me?'

'Well, I said I'd *help* . . .'

'Oh, Jess, you're a star!' Rubellina flung her arms around Jessica, then pushed the new shoes and the ribbons into her hands. 'We're friends forever!'

'We're really friends now?' asked Jessica, pleased despite herself.

'Of course! But Jessie, I must dash. I have to run to the Minister's Offices to say goodnight to Daddy.'

And with that, Rubellina was gone.

That evening, Jessica sat on her bed sewing Rubellina's ribbons on while Sinbad sat opposite making loud *harrumph* noises. Eventually she snapped at him.

'Sinbad, you're distracting me!'

Sinbad's ears twitched, the way they only did when he was really angry. 'Jessica, Rubellina's made you her servant, and you don't even care!'

'I just want to get along with everyone,' Jessica said. 'If that means helping Rubellina, then that's that. Besides, I'm sure she'd help me with something *she's* better at.'

'Being a meanie-beanie,' huffed Sinbad. 'That's the *only* thing Rubellina

Goodfellow is better at.'

But the next day, Rubellina was sweet to Jessica when the shoes were handed over. She gave her a huge bag of Lemon Fizzicles and said how much fun they'd have together at the big rehearsal that evening.

That evening, Mistress Camomile came along to the rehearsal, to see how the

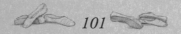

Beginners' preparations were going.

'We will begin with the dance of the forest sprites,' Mustard Stockings announced. 'Rubellina, are you ready for your solo in the middle?'

Rubellina nodded as she tied up her new shoes.

Jessica, Crys and Laura-Bella watched happily as Valentina, the chief forest sprite, led the dance. Even stern Mr Melchior the tiger looked impressed, and Olympia, Valentina's eagle, cried so many tears of joy that Pollux's soft furry fox-tail had to be used to mop them up.

Rubellina's entrance came just after Valentina had performed a clever little series of solo steps. Olympia was so excited by Valentina's solo that she flew up into the air, squawking in delight. Just as she did so, Rubellina danced on for her solo.

But with her first pirouette, Rubellina's ballet shoe flew right off. It sailed high through the air, hitting

Olympia smack in the beak.

The eagle dropped like a stone to the floor.

'Olympia!' cried Valentina.

Everyone gathered round, but Olympia was knocked out cold. Valentina

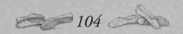

wailed, Sinbad wailed even louder, and Mistress Camomile sent her pet leopard running to fetch the King's own Doctor.

When the Doctor had come and taken Olympia and Valentina away, promising that the eagle would be quite all right, Mistress Camomile picked Rubellina's flying ballet shoe up from the floor.

'Rubellina! What were you thinking? Your ribbons were *loose*!'

'Loose?' gasped Rubellina. 'They

couldn't have been!'

Mistress Camomile waved the shoe at Rubellina. Both ribbons had come off

completely, leaving only loose threads behind. 'This is extremely dangerous, Rubellina! Ballerinas must *always* sew their ribbons on properly, or accidents happen. You should know that.'

'But I didn't sew them. *Jessica did!*' Rubellina announced loudly. 'Jessica, I thought we were friends! Is this *another* one of your practical jokes?'

'I sewed those ribbons on perfectly!' Jessica protested. But then she thought back to the previous evening. Sinbad had been distracting her . . . had she *really* done a proper job? 'I mean . . . I *thought* I did…'

'Jessica, I am ashamed of you!' Mistress Camomile's voice shook. 'I am giving you a second Black Mark.'

Everybody gasped.

'Oh, please, give *me* the Black Mark instead,' begged Sinbad. 'It was my fault, I was so angry with Jess, she wasn't concentrating!'

'Quiet, Sinbad! Quiet, everyone! The rehearsal is over.' And with that, Mistress

Camomile left the hall.

Rubellina turned to Jessica, reached into her bag to snatch back the Lemon Fizzicles, and flounced off. Everyone else followed, until only Jessica, Crys and Laura-Bella were left.

'Do you think Valentina will ever forgive me?' Jessica asked, swamped with misery.

'Val wasn't angry, just upset about Olympia,' said Crys, squeezing Jessica's arm.

'She knows it was an accident,' added Laura-Bella, kindly.

'Another Black Mark!' Mr Melchior sounded disapproving, but he patted Jessica kindly with his paw. 'Oh, Jessica, you must be *extremely* careful now . . .'

Olympia made a swift recovery, and was thrilled when Sinbad spent a whole day tending her, telling her stories to pass the time. Luckily Laura-Bella was right, and Valentina was not angry with

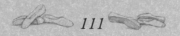

Jessica in the least.

'It was an accident, Jess,' she said. 'Besides, Olympia's fine.'

'If there's anything I can do to make it up to you . . .' said Jessica.

Valentina grinned. 'Just check your ribbons before you go onstage! You mustn't knock the Queen senseless with a flying shoe tomorrow night.'

Jessica laughed, but she could not shake off a dreadful feeling in the pit of her stomach. *Two black marks* in her first

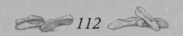

term! It was not how she had imagined things at all.

'I've just got to give the best performance I can,' she told herself, practising her steps whenever she could. 'Then I can start afresh next term!'

Jessica's stomach was so knotted up with these worries that she almost forgot to be nervous about the dress rehearsal that evening. She only remembered what was happening when her classmates began packing up their books early in History of Ballet.

'Early supper tonight, Jess,' said Crys. 'We've got to start our hair and make-up!'

'Jessica, would you stay behind?' called Master Silas, as the other girls filed out of the classroom. 'I hear you've been in a bit of trouble.'

Jessica hung her head. 'Things haven't gone exactly as I planned.'

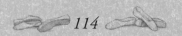

Master Silas sighed, and sat down quite suddenly behind his desk. He rubbed his left leg, the leg that made him limp, as though it was aching more than usual. 'You know, Jessica, Rubellina's father was a pupil at the boys' ballet school at the same time as me,' Master Silas said.

'Chancellor Goodfellow?' Jessica asked, politely. She wondered why he was telling her this.

'Yes. He disliked me from the very start.' Master Silas had a faraway look in his eyes. 'They are clever people, those Goodfellows. Still, they are not quite as clever as they *think* they are . . .'

Jessica shifted from foot to foot, wishing Master Silas would just let her go so that she could eat her early supper.

'You're a smart girl, Jessica. Don't let anyone convince you things are your fault when you *know* they're not.' Master Silas stood, and limped towards the door. 'Good luck tonight, Jessica.

Oh . . .' he suddenly added, '. . . and be careful.'

It was exciting to go through the stage doors into the Theatre. Beginners were dashing about pulling costumes on, and older girls chased after them to do their hair and make-up. Jessica hurried to her peg in the dressing room and changed into her first costume, a plain grey

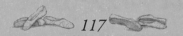

chiffon dress with matching ballet shoes.

'Jessica!' Sinbad suddenly yelped. 'Your skirt!'

Jessica glanced down at her costume, and cried out.

The grey skirt was covered with sticky patches of bright red.

'Is this . . . ?'

'*Blood?*' gasped Sinbad, letting out a bray so loud Jessica was sure it must have been heard all the way back home in the Rocks.

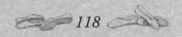

'Paint!' sighed Jessica, staring at the red stains that were now all over her hands too. 'I was going to say *paint*.'

'Oh,' said Sinbad. 'Well, that's nowhere *near* as exciting.'

'I must have touched something wet,' wailed Jessica. 'All that scenery sitting about newly painted . . .' She sighed. 'I'll have to wash it out later.'

'Better wash your hands *now*,' advised Sinbad, before trotting off to see if he could persuade anyone to dress him

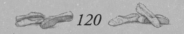

up as the Fairy God-Donkey.

Jessica scrubbed at her hands and skirt, but the red stains wouldn't come out. Then she hurried to have her hair and make-up done, shooing Sinbad away from the mirror where he was having his long nose powdered with an enormous pink puff.

'Jess, you look great!' Crys sat at the next mirror with Pollux as her blonde hair was pinned up beneath her Prince's velvet cap. 'You'd better hurry,' she added. 'Mustard Stockings was just shouting for you.'

Jessica hurried towards the stage, past the scenery leaning against the brick walls. There was the giant pumpkin that came onstage at the end of the first act. There were all the fir trees for the forest scene. There was the fairy carriage that the Fairy Godmother would make her entrance on . . .

And there was a shadowy figure climbing down the steps of the fairy carriage. A figure dressed in a silver fairy costume, with blonde ringlets.

Rubellina.

Rubellina jumped when she bumped into Jessica. 'Just checking the carriage is ready for my big entrance,' she said, tossing her hair.

Jessica was about to reply when a yell came from the stage.

'*Jessica Juniper!*' came Mustard

Stockings' voice. 'Where are you?'

'I'd better go. Good luck, Rubellina,' Jessica added, trying to be nice. But Rubellina flounced away without replying.

Out on the stage, the lights made Jessica blink, and she could see little of the famous red-and-gold theatre apart from Mustard Stockings and Mistress Odette in the front. She hoped they would not notice the red stains on her costume. As the orchestra began to play,

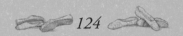

Jessica took her very first steps on the stage of the Palace Theatre.

Then, from behind the stage, there came a terrible scream.

Jessica stopped dancing. The orchestra stopped playing. Everybody ran backstage.

Rubellina was lying beside the fairy carriage, clutching her leg. Red paint was dripping down the carriage steps.

'There was paint,' Rubellina gasped. 'I slipped . . . My leg is broken!'

'Lie still!' ordered Mistress Odette.

Beginners gathered around, and Rubellina's eagle flapped about, squawking more furiously than ever.

'But who would have done such a

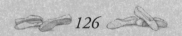

thing?' wept Rubellina. 'Who poured paint over my carriage steps?'

'Don't be silly!' said Mistress Odette. 'This was an accident.'

'Jessica was the last person I saw near my carriage . . .' gasped Rubellina.

'I didn't . . . I wasn't . . . I *wouldn't*,' Jessica began, but Mistress Odette silenced her with one look.

'If this is a practical joke too far . . .'

'Mistress Odette, I had nothing to do with the paint!'

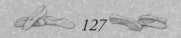

Rubellina took a deep breath. Something like a smile flickered over her face.

'Then why,' she asked, in a small, sorrowful voice, 'is Jessica *covered in red paint*?'

There was a long, dreadful silence.

Then Mistress Odette got to her feet. 'Jessica,' she said. 'Show me your hands.'

Unable to speak, Jessica held out her bright red palms.

'I am sorry to say this,' Mistress

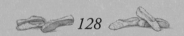 *128*

Odette said, 'but I am giving you a third Black Mark. You, Jessica Juniper, are expelled.'

CHAPTER NINE
Friend in Need

Jessica pretended to be asleep when her friends came up to bed after the dress rehearsal. She could not face any of them. Besides, Sinbad did all the talking she needed.

'Mistress Odette's sending us away tomorrow morning,' the donkey sobbed. 'Jessica's packed our bags and everything!'

'We can't let this happen!' Jessica heard Laura-Bella say. 'Jess didn't spill that paint. We know she didn't!'

'But how can we prove it?' Crys whispered. 'She was caught red-handed! Rubellina's done a fine job this time. This was all because Jess got the part Rubellina wanted in the show. And now Rubellina's got her way.'

'What do you mean?' asked Sinbad.

'After Mistress Odette took you two away, Rubellina made a remarkable recovery,' said Laura-Bella. 'She said her leg felt fine after all. Then Mustard Stockings said someone else would have to play Cinderella, and he gave her the part.'

Jessica stifled a sob.

'Rubellina planned it all.' Valentina and Olympia were crying too. 'What are we going to do?'

'What *can* we do? Rubellina's the

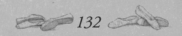

Chancellor's daughter! Nobody will believe us.'

'Let's go to bed,' said Mr Melchior, 'and work out what to do in the morning. There's nothing we can do at this hour, and we'll be no help to Jessica if we're sleepy-headed tomorrow.'

This was sound advice, and the girls were exhausted. One by one, they all got into bed. Eventually their breathing steadied, and they slept.

But Jessica could not fall asleep. She was too worried about how her family would feel when she arrived home in disgrace. She tossed and turned beneath her quilt, getting more hot and bothered as every minute ticked by.

Then she heard something. Somebody was getting out of bed.

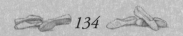

Jessica peeked over her quilt just in time to see Ursula hurrying out of the dormitory. She was fully clothed and her bear was wrapped around her neck. She was also carrying her suitcase.

Jessica threw off her quilt.

'Jessica?' Sinbad was awake in an instant, his long ears standing on end.

'Sssh, Sinbad!'

'Where are you going?' Sinbad watched her pull her clothes on over her pyjamas, and stuff her feet into her outdoor shoes. 'Are we leaving *already*?'

'No!' Jessica whispered. 'Sinbad, go back to sleep.'

Sinbad clattered across the dormitory after her. 'Have you got an idea? Because I've got plans for revenge too, you know. There's that custard-in-the-shoes trick, or I could just kick Rubellina really hard in the shins, or –'

'We're not going to get revenge, Sinbad,' whispered Jessica, knowing that there was no way she could shake him off now. 'We're going to stop Ursula from running away.'

'Why is Ursula running away?'

'I think she knows what Rubellina did with that paint.'

'And she hasn't even the courage to come forward? We have to stop her!'

Jessica leapt up on his back, something she only did in an emergency. She held tightly on to Sinbad's ears as the donkey raced down the stairs, taking them four at a time and missing out the

last few altogether. They sped through the Winter Garden, Jessica ducking under the low branches of the weeping willow trees. Then they raced towards the huge oak doors that would lead out of the Palace – the door Ursula must have just used.

But only a short distance from the doors, a Royal Guard leapt out of the shadows.

'In the name of the King, who goes there?'

'Please let us past!' begged Jessica.

'In the name of the King, go back to bed!'

'But please, it's my only chance to stop being expelled!'

'In the name of the King,' said the guard, 'sorry to hear that.'

Jessica knew that they would never get past him. 'Come on, Sinbad. Let's go back to bed.'

Heads down, Sinbad's so low that his ears brushed the floor, they began to walk back towards the Winter Garden.

'Well, I suppose at least we weren't executed,' Sinbad sighed, as they passed the classrooms.

Jessica could see a light from under Master Silas's door. Hushing Sinbad, she pricked up her ears.

'There's someone in there, Sinbad!'

They pressed their ears up against the classroom door.

'Thank you for coming to me, Ursula.' It was Master Silas. 'I'll see that everything works out all right.'

'But I should be expelled,' said Ursula, sounding miserable. 'You should send me home. I went along with Rubellina's horrible plan because I was scared of her. That doesn't make me a very worthy Ballerina.'

'You've done the right thing now,' said Master Silas, soothingly. 'I think we can save Jessica from being expelled.'

'Hurrah!' shouted Sinbad, forgetting himself entirely.

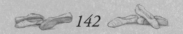 *142*

The classroom door opened swiftly.

'Sinbad! Jessica!' Master Silas smiled. 'What a pleasant midnight surprise. But shouldn't you be in bed?'

Jessica suspected that she could not be in any more trouble than she was already. 'Sorry, Master Silas. I thought Ursula was running away. I didn't know she was coming to own up.'

'I'm very sorry, Jessica,' Ursula began. But she didn't have a chance to say any more, because Jessica threw her arms around her.

'Thank you, Ursula, thank you!' said Jessica. Ursula looked amazed. Then Jessica turned to Master Silas. 'Will I be allowed to stay now?'

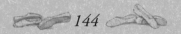

Master Silas looked very serious. 'I will speak to Mistress Odette in the morning. I am sure she will believe that pouring paint around backstage is a very old trick of the Goodfellows.'

Jessica's mind went back to the strange things Master Silas had said earlier that day, in his classroom. She remembered the sad, faraway look in his eyes, and the fact that his bad leg had seemed to be hurting more than usual when he spoke of Chancellor

Goodfellow. Suddenly she realised how his old injury might have happened. 'Master Silas,' she asked, 'did Rubellina's father play a paint-spilling trick on you when you were at school?'

Master Silas grimaced. 'It was a long time ago. But yes, my hopes of being a dancer were put to an end by a little . . . accident. Of course, nobody believed me then, but it is not too late for me to save another dancer,' said Master Silas. 'Now, girls, go to bed, and

trust that I will make everything right
by the morning.'

CHAPTER TEN
Friends Indeed

Crys, Laura-Bella and Valentina were glumly eating their breakfast at their usual table, when suddenly Olympia let out a squawk.

'It's Jessica and Sinbad!'

The entire Banqueting Hall fell silent as Jessica and Sinbad walked in, their heads held high. Behind them walked Ursula with her bear, Dorothea. They both stared shyly at the floor.

'What's Jessica doing here?' came the whispers from all around. 'Wasn't she expelled?'

'Jess, over here,' hissed Crys, waving her friend over. 'Everybody's staring!'

'Let them,' said Jessica. 'I haven't done anything wrong.'

'*We* know that,' said Laura-Bella, not even noticing that Sinbad had begun to tuck into her plate of Snowberry Waffles. 'But you've been expelled, Jess.'

'Actually,' Jessica said with a grin, 'I haven't been expelled after all.' She turned to Ursula, who was standing nervously nearby. 'Come and eat, Ursula. You must be starving! Ursula's had a rather horrid time,' she continued. 'You see –'

'Ssssh!' hissed Sinbad, sputtering waffle everywhere. 'Here comes Rubellina!'

Now every single girl in the dining
room was staring as Rubellina walked
towards Jessica's table.

'She's going to throw her juice at
her . . .'

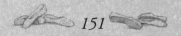

'She's going to pull her hair . . .'

Rubellina's face was purple with fury. 'I'm here to apologise, Jessica,' she said, through gritted teeth.

A gasp ran around the Hall.

'I tried to make it look like you wanted to hurt me, Jessica. But it was me who did it all, even the red paint.' Rubellina scowled. 'I'm very sorry.'

'Thanks, Rubellina,' Jessica said. 'Let's be friends.'

She put out her hand for Rubellina

to shake. Rubellina took it, scowling, then stalked away, her eagle squawking loudly.

Ignoring the stares, Jessica grinned at her friends. 'You see?' she said. 'I told you everything was all right. And I'd like Ursula to be our friend now, if nobody minds. She isn't friends with Rubellina any more.'

'I never really was,' whispered Ursula.

'We'd love you to be our friend,' said Laura-Bella, squeezing Ursula's hand.

'I'd love it, too,' said Ursula, with a shy smile.

'And I'd love it, too,' said Dorothea, Ursula's bear, in the first words the girls had ever heard her speak.

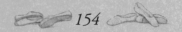

'And *I'd* love it most of all!' announced Sinbad, gazing around happily at everyone and waggling his ears. 'The more the merrier, I say.' He looked hopefully at Jessica. 'Celebration Flancakes all round?' he asked.

It was lucky that the End-of-term Ballet was that night, because the Beginners were all too excited to keep talking about the scandal for long. Jessica and her friends were so nervous about the performance that they could hardly concentrate on lessons all day. Matters became even more extraordinary when Sinbad dashed up to them in the dormitory after lunch. He was out of breath.

'Jessica, Jessica, you won't believe it!' he gasped. 'Mistress Camomile just called me to her classroom to tell me that Rubellina's been banned from the show tonight because of what she did to you. Her part in the show has to be played by someone else. And guess who Mistress

Camomile has chosen!'

Jessica stared at him. '*You?*'

Sinbad spun a wild pirouette. 'I'm the Fairy God-Donkey after all!'

And that evening, despite Sinbad's loud clip-clopping, the ballet was a huge success.

Crys, Laura-Bella, Valentina and Ursula pushed Jessica and Sinbad out on to the stage by themselves for a solo curtain call, watching in delight as the audience cheered and applauded their

friend. Nobody clapped louder than Master Silas, in the front row, and Jessica nodded at him as she swept into her finest curtsey.

'You know,' she whispered to Sinbad, as they took their final bow, 'I think we belong at the Royal Ballet School after all.'

THE END

Glossary

Cinnamon Twists: Long, thin doughnuts that are twisted into a double knot before being freshly fried and then sprinkled with cinnamon sugar. A speciality of Silverberg. Donkeys love them.

Crocodils and Daffodaisies: Crocodils are yellow or purple wild flowers that grow in spring all over the Kingdom. In fact, wild flowers is a good description — like the crocodiles they sound like, the flowers will give you a little nip on the hand if you try to pick them before they are ready. Daffodaisies are less dangerous. They are tall white-and-yellow daisies the size of daffodils, and perfect for making into long Daffodaisy chains.

Frosting-Stones: Precious stones mined from the Frosty Mountains themselves. They come in several colours — red, green, blue and a deep amber — but the most prized of all are the colourless stones, more beautiful even than our own diamonds. The stones come out of the mountain just as they are, with no need for cutting or polishing. Finding a particularly large Frosting-Stone could make your fortune, but mining them is dangerous and difficult work.

Hot Buttered Flumpets: These are a little bit like the crumpets you eat for tea, but they taste softer and slightly sweeter, and they are shaped like fingers. They are always served piping hot, with melted butter oozing through the holes.

Ice Buns: Made for special occasions in the Lakes, these buns look plain on the outside but are filled with creamy pink-and-white ice cream on the inside. Be careful when you bite in!

Iced White Chocolate Drops: An expensive treat that only the very rich can afford. These chocolate drops are found by divers inside seashells at the very bottom of the northern Lake. They stay ice-cold right up until they are popped into your mouth, where they slowly melt.

Icicle Bicycles: Quite simply, bicycles carved from blocks of ice. They are the best way to travel from one side of the

frozen Lake to the other, as the icy wheels speed you across without any danger of skidding or slipping. But be warned, and pack a cushion — or the icy seat will leave your bottom extremely cold.

Lemon Fizzicles: Lemon-flavoured chewy sweets that fizz with tiny bubbles when you suck them.

Raspberry Flancakes: Flancakes are yeasty, flaky pancakes that rise up to five

or ten centimetres thick when you cook them in a special Flancake pan. Their outside is brown and rich with butter, their inside light and airy. Flancakes can be made in any flavour, but raspberry is the most popular. Donkeys love them, too.

Scoffins: Halfway between a scone and a muffin. They are best served fresh from the oven, split in two, and spread with Snowberry Jam.

Snowberries: Round, plump, juicy berries that grow in hedgerows all over the Kingdom throughout the winter. The snowberries from the south and the west are very dark pink, while the ones that grow in the east and the north are red in colour. Snowberries are always eaten cooked – in jams, Flancakes, waffles or muffins – where they taste sweet but tart at the same time. Don't make the mistake of eating one straight from the hedgerow, however tasty it looks.

Uncooked Snowberries are delicious, but they pop open in your mouth and fill it with a juice so sticky that your teeth are instantly glued together. This can take a whole morning to wear off.

SpringSprung Day: The official first day of spring, and a big day for the inhabitants of the Kingdom after a long, cold winter. SpringSprung Day is marked with a big festival in Silverberg, but the Valley Dwellers throw parties in

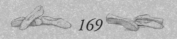

their own homes for those who would rather not travel the long way to the City. For many, the highlight of the festivities is the SpringSprung Pudding (see below), though many delicious delicacies are served, including lemon-and-orangeade.

SpringSprung Pudding: *A sponge pudding, filled with plump currants and chewy dried Snowberries, this is steamed in a huge pudding basin and served in thick slices, sprinkled with*

sugar, on SpringSprung Day. One pudding will normally feed ten hungry people. Sinbad can eat a whole pudding all by himself, with room for afters.

Toffee Apple Torte: The speciality of the Grand Café and Tea-Rooms in Silverberg. This tart is made with delicate slices of the fruits that grow in the toffee-apple orchards in the deep south of the Valley, then served warm with toffee-butter sauce.

Who's Who in the Kingdom of the Frosty Mountains

The girls and their pets

Jessica Juniper – *Ballerina from the western Rocks*

Sinbad – *Jessica's pet donkey*

Crystal Coldwater – *Ballerina from the northern Lake*

Pollux – *Crystal's pet white fox*

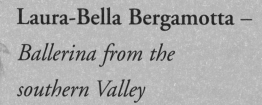

Laura-Bella Bergamotta – *Ballerina from the southern Valley*

Mr Melchior – *Laura-Bella's pet tiger*

Ursula of the Boughs – *Ballerina from the eastern Forest*

Dorothea – *Ursula's pet bear*

Valentina de la Frou – *Ballerina from the City*

Olympia – *Valentina's pet eagle*

Some other Ballerinas

Rubellina Goodfellow – *Ballerina from the City, and the Chancellor's daughter*

Jo-Jo Marshall – *Another Ballerina from the City, and Rubellina's best friend*

The Teachers

Mistress Odette – *the Headmistress*

Mistress Camomile – *a Ballet teacher*

Master Lysander – *another Ballet teacher, also known as Mustard Stockings*

Master Silas – *the History of Ballet teacher*

Mistress Hawthorne – *the Gym teacher*

Mistress Babette – *the Costume, Hair and Make-up teacher*

Master Jacques – *the Mime teacher*

The Royal Party

King Caspar – *the King*

Queen Mab – *the Queen*

Chancellor Godwin Goodfellow –
the Kingdom's Chancellor

Don't miss the second book in the series

Crystal Coldwater

The Ballerinas-in-Training are excited –
they have to write about their favourite
ballerina, Eva Snowdrop. So why is Crys
so upset? Even her fox, Pollux, can't
soothe her. Can the girls find out? And
how will Icicle Bicycles help?

**Twinkle your toes with the Ballerinas
and their talking pets!**

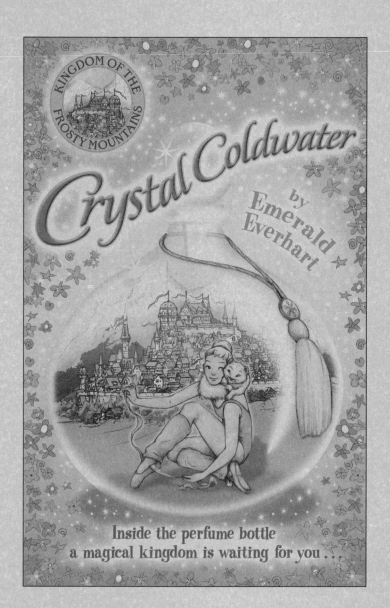

KINGDOM OF THE FROSTY MOUNTAINS

Crystal Coldwater

by
Emerald
Everhart

Inside the perfume bottle
a magical kingdom is waiting for you...

EGMONT PRESS: ETHICAL PUBLISHING

Egmont Press is about turning writers into successful authors and children into passionate readers – producing books that enrich and entertain. As a responsible children's publisher, we go even further, considering the world in which our consumers are growing up.

Safety First
Naturally, all of our books meet legal safety requirements. But we go further than this; every book with play value is tested to the highest standards – if it fails, it's back to the drawing-board.

Made Fairly
We are working to ensure that the workers involved in our supply chain – the people that make our books – are treated with fairness and respect.

Responsible Forestry
We are committed to ensuring all our papers come from environmentally and socially responsible forest sources.

For more information, please visit our website at
www.egmont.co.uk/ethicalpublishing